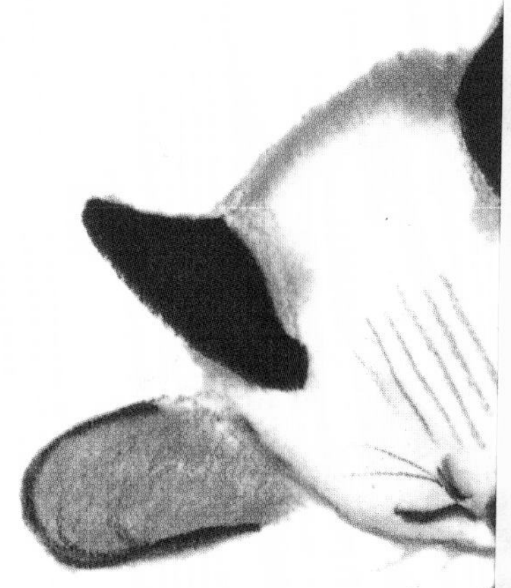

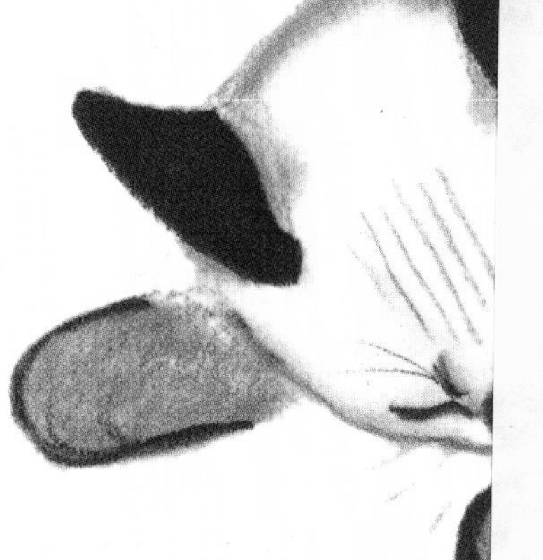

BABETTE

BABETTE

Story and Pictures by
CLARE TURLAY NEWBERRY

Babette's father had a wide kind face

First SMITHMARK edition, 1999

This edition published in 1999 by SMITHMARK Publishers, a division of U.S. Media Holdings, Inc., 115 West 18th Street, New York, NY 10011.

SMITHMARK books are available for bulk purchase for sales promotion and premium use. For details write or call the manager of special sales, SMITHMARK Publishers, 115 West 18th Street, New York, NY 10011; 212-519-1300.

Library of Congress Catalog Card Number: 98–75099
ISBN: 0–7651–0950–6

Printed in Hong Kong
10987654321

To
Doris Bryant

Babette

ONCE there was a little girl named Charity, only she was called Chatty, for short. She went to school, of course, for she was eight years old, but on Saturdays she stayed at home by herself.

Every Saturday morning her mother kissed her good-bye and said, "Be a good girl, darling. And don't forget to eat your lunch." Then she caught a tube and went off to business. So Chatty was left to play all by herself, and she got very lonely.

One Saturday not long before Christmas she was even lonelier than usual. She had cut out all the paper-doll ladies she could find in her mother's old magazines, and it was still morning.

"I *wish* I had somebody to play with," sighed Chatty as she picked up the scraps of paper from her doll-cutting.

And then she heard a funny noise. It was at the door of the room, down near the floor. Scratch . . . scratch . . . scratch . . . Chatty kept very still and listened.

There it was again. Scratch . . . scratch . . . scratch. And then a faint *mew!* Chatty jumped up and threw open the door.

"*Oh!*" she exclaimed in delight. For there on the threshold, looking wistfully up at her, sat a tiny kitten.

"You *sweet* little thing!" cried Chatty, picking her up. "Haven't you got any home or any mother?" The kitten did not answer, but she purred politely and bumped her soft head against Chatty's cheek.

She was a rather queer-looking kitten, Chatty thought, and so very small. Most of her was creamy white, but her little nose, ears, paws, and tail were brown.

"I've seen black kitties trimmed in white, and grey kitties trimmed in black," Chatty thought, holding the kitten against her ear to listen to the purring, "but I never did see a white kitty trimmed in brown like this one."

However, she had a sweet face and pretty blue eyes, and she was such a soft, cuddly little thing that Chatty loved her at once.

"Never mind, kitty," she said, tenderly. "You can stay here and be my cat." For hadn't her mother promised just the other day that she might have a kitten?

The first thing, of course, was to find a good name for her. Chatty repeated all the nice names she could think of, to see how they sounded. She tried Alice and Heidi and Wendy and Shirley Temple and lots of others but not one of them seemed to fit.

At last she thought of Babette, and *it* fitted perfectly. So she named the kitten Babette.

"And now, Babette," said Chatty, gently putting her down. "if you'll wait just a minute I'll get you some lunch." For the alarm clock on the desk said almost twelve o'clock.

She got the bottle of milk in from the window sill, where it was keeping cold and fresh for her own lunch. Then standing on tiptoe, she reached down a blue-and-white saucer from the big cupboard. She poured some milk into it, very carefully, while Babette watched her and mewed for her to hurry.

But when the dish was set on the floor Babette took only one sip. Then she backed away, shaking her little head.

"*Mew!*" she said, crossly.

"Don't you like milk, Babette?" asked Chatty, anxiously. She pushed the saucer toward the kitten and tried to make her drink, but Babbette would not touch the milk again. She just went on mewing.

Then Chatty thought of something. Perhaps the milk was too cold for so young a kitten. Perhaps it should be

Babette felt
playful now

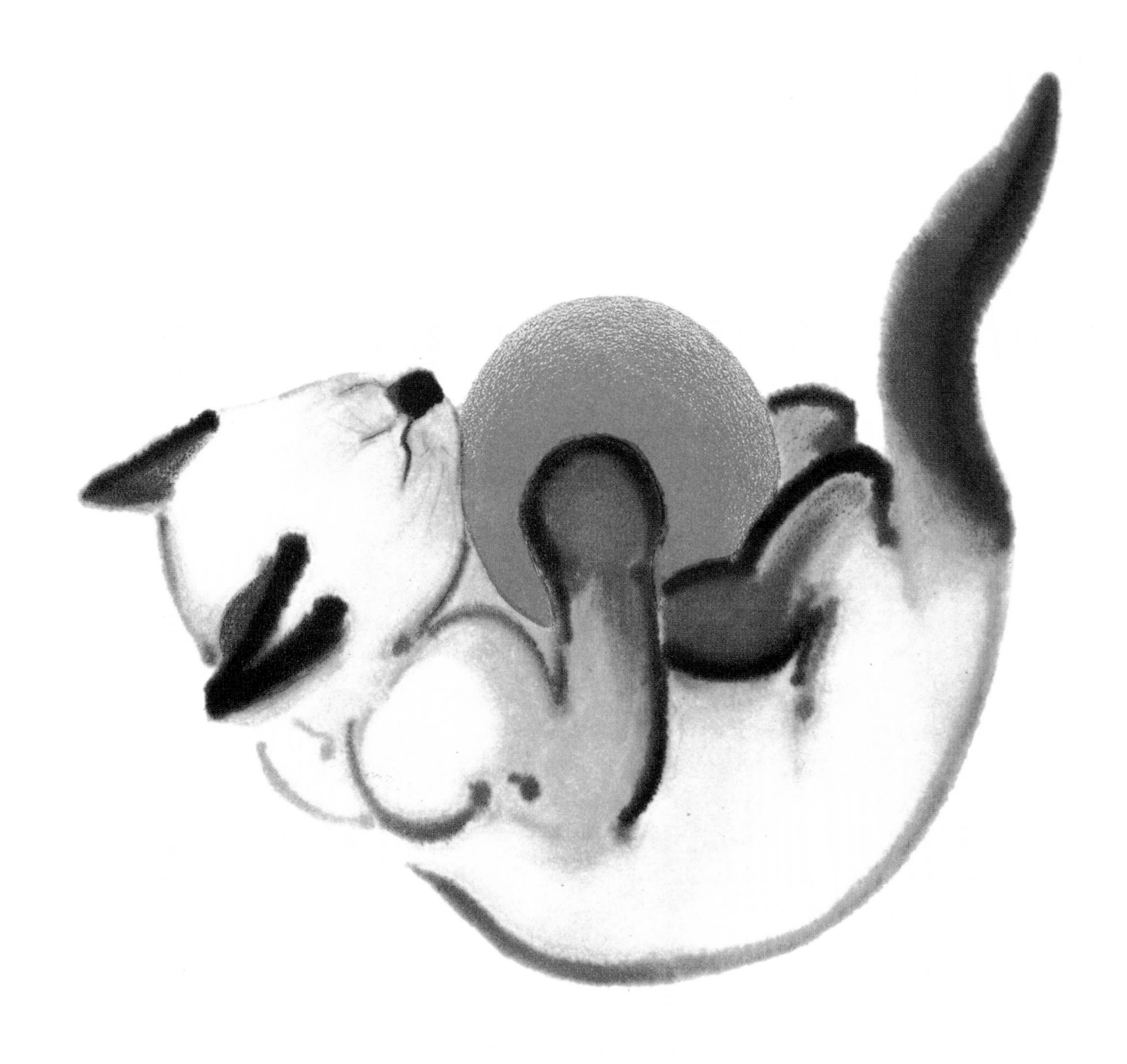

She pounced on the rubber
ball and fought it

warmed for her. In the cupboard was the electric plate Chatty's mother cooked on. All you had to do was turn the knob underneath it and the wires inside became a lovely bright red. But Chatty was not allowed to turn on the power unless her mother was there and said she might.

"Oh dear!" said Chatty, aloud. "What shall I do?"

And her question was answered in a very strange way.

The Radiator in the corner suddenly gave a long-drawn-out *whooooooooosh!* For a moment Chatty stared at it. Then she giggled. Once more she ran to the cupboard, got a saucepan, poured the milk from the saucer into it, and set it on the hot radiator.

In a few minutes the milk was warm. And this time when it was put before Babette she drank it hungrily, her tiny tongue going *slap, slap, slap,* until the dish was empty.

While Babette washed herself beside the radiator Chatty made her own lunch, a big sandwich and a glass of milk. When she had finished eating she washed the dishes, dried them nicely, and put them back in the cupboard, just as her mother liked her to do.

Babette felt playful now. She began to scamper about the room, patting things with her little brown paws and jumping sideways stiff legged. She seemed to think everything in the room was alive, from the table legs to Chatty's bedroom slippers. And when she found a rubber ball on the floor she pounced upon it and fought it, with such a fierce look on her baby face that Chatty could not help laughing.

After a while Babette got tired, for she was just a baby. She curled up on Chatty's lap and purred herself to sleep,

and Chatty sat very still for a long time so as not to awaken her.

Chatty must almost have gone to sleep herself, for she jumped when she heard her mother's key in the lock.

"Oh, Mother, Mother, Mother, look what I've got!" she called, holding up Babette, who began to purr again drowsily without bothering to open her eyes. "May I keep her, Mother, *may* I?"

"Good gracious!" said her mother, as she laid down her bundles from the grocer's shop and began to take off her hat and coat, "What a funny-looking kitten! Where on earth did you find her?"

"She just came and scratched on our door this morning," Chatty explained, eagerly. "She hasn't any home, Mother, she's just a little orphan kitty. *May* I keep her?"

"But, darling," said her mother, putting on her apron, "suppose she belongs to someone? She doesn't look like a stray cat to me. She is too clean and gentle."

She looked hard at Babette.

"Chatty—I believe that's a Siamese kitten! And if it is, it must belong to someone. Siamese cats are expensive."

"Oh, Mother," wailed Chatty, who had never heard of a Siamese cat before, "*please* don't say that! *Please* let me keep her!"

At that moment someone knocked at the door. And when her mother opened it a tall, worried young man stood in the doorway. He was Mr. Todd from the flat upstairs, he explained, and he was looking for a small Siamese kitten. The woman who came in to clean must have let the kitten

out, he said, for when he got home from work she was gone.

Then he saw Babette in Chatty's arms.

"Oh, there she is!" he exclaimed with relief.

"She came to our door this morning," Chatty's mother said, "and my little girl has played with her all day.... Give the kitten to Mr. Todd, darling."

"I don't know what I'm going to do about that charwoman," said Mr. Todd. "Last Saturday it was the kitten's mother that got out, I can't tell you how grateful I am to your little girl for taking care of the kitten."

"Charity," said her mother again, "give Mr. Todd the kitten!"

Chatty started slowly toward the door with Babette snuggled close against her downcast cheek. The tears which had been brimming in her eyes began to spill over. Mr. Todd looked at her and said, quickly:

"Perhaps the little girl would like to take the kitten back to the mother cat herself. Has she ever seen a Siamese cat before?"

"No, I don't believe she has " replied Chatty's mother. "You may go with Mr. Todd and see the big cat, Chatty, but come straight back. Dinner will be ready in a minute."

As Chatty followed Mr. Todd along the hall she heard a cat yowling mournfully.

"MrrOWrrh! MrrOWrrh! MrrOWrrh!" it went, over and over and over.

"That's Cellophane, the kitten's mother. She's crying for her child," said Mr. Todd as he unlocked the door.

The yowls stopped as the door opened, and Cellophane leaped from the floor and landed on Mr. Todd's shoulder.

"It's all right, Cellophane, we've found her," he said, soothingly. He unhooked Cellophane's claws from his coat and set her down. At the same time Babette scrambled loose from Chatty and tumbled to the floor beside her mother.

"*Prrrt! Prrrt!*" said Cellophane, joyfully, sniffing her child to see if she was all right. Babette nuzzled her mother eagerly, and Cellophane began to wash her with her rough pink tongue, making tender little scolding noises in her throat.

"Cellophane is talking cat language," said Chatty shyly. "She's telling the kitten she was naughty to run away." She rubbed her eyes with the back of her hand and tried to smile.

Cellophane was darker than Babette, for Siamese cats are born white and get darker as they grow up. Instead of only a brown smudge on her nose, Cellophane's whole face was brown, and her big blue eyes were as beautiful as jewels. She was, Chatty decided, a sort of butterscotch-pudding-coloured kitty, trimmed in chocolate.

"And this is the kitten's father," said Mr. Todd with a grin, handing Chatty a photograph of a large handsome cat with a wide kind face. "He lives at someone else's house, so we just have his picture. . . . And now, Chatty, perhaps you had better run home to your dinner. You may come and see the cats again some other time."

So Chatty had to say good-bye to Babette and go sadly back to her own room, kittenless.

After that, every night when Mr. Todd got home from work he found Chatty waiting for him on the stairs, hoping for another glimpse of Babette. So one day he said:

"Chatty, how would you like to take care of my cats on Saturdays? Then you would have a whole day with that kitten, and I shouldn't have to worry about the charwoman letting them out."

Of course Chatty was delighted. So after that Mr. Todd stopped on Saturday mornings with a cat under each arm and a package of chopped meat in his coat pocket. And every Saturday night at dinner time he stopped again, and took his cats home with him.

He even called the kitten Babette, for he hadn't had time to name her himself, he said, and Babette was as good a name as any. So now Chatty could hardly wait for Saturday to come, and she wasn't lonely any more.

One wintry afternoon, coming in from school, Chatty met Alberto in the hall. Alberto looked after the furnace, and mended the lights when they went out, and everything like that. He and Chatty were good friends.

"Hello, Chatty!" he greeted her. "Cold weather, huh? Well, it'll soon be Christmas!"

"Only three more days, Mr. Alberto," said Chatty, happily, stamping the snow off her galoshes, "and we're going to have a tree and everything! Mother got me a present to give to Babette—it's a catnip mouse, but don't you go and tell her!"

Alberto laughed loudly at the idea of his telling Babette. He knew all about Chatty's taking care of Mr. Todd's cats.

"What'll you do when that young fellow goes away?" he demanded, teasingly. "You going to get yourself another cat, perhaps?"

Chatty stared at him round eyed.

"Yes," said Alberto. "Didn't he tell you yet? That fellow's going away after Christmas. He's got a job."

Chatty gave him a horrified look and without another word turned and ran up the stairs. Inside the room she flung herself on the bed and cried bitterly.

Presently her mother came home and was told the sad news. She washed Chatty's face, and got her a drink of water and a fresh hanky from the chest-of-drawers. Then she said, quietly:

"Chatty, I can't afford to buy you a Siamese cat, much as I'd like to. But I will get you a nice plain kitten as soon as I possibly can. There are some darling ones at the A & P —black with white noses. I'm almost sure the grocer would give us one."

But Chatty only cried the harder. And not even thinking about Christmas could make her feel much better.

Christmas was certainly very near. The butcher's and grocer's shops across the street were full of people buying their turkeys and plum puddings, and the pavements in front were heaped with holly and mistletoe and Christmas trees. And all day long in every shop and tea-room the wireless was playing "Silent Night."

Chatty's mother got some pretty sprigs of holly and decorated the room. And every night when she came home from work she brought one or two packages that she didn't

unwrap, but put away mysteriously on the top shelf of the clothes cupboard.

But Chatty was too miserable to care very much what was in them. Every night before dinner she waited for Mr. Todd on the stairs, but he never seemed to come home any more. So she had no chance to ask him if she might borrow Babette just once more.

At last it was really Christmas Eve. Chatty hung her stocking—one of the long ones—from the mantelpiece. Then she lay in bed and watched her mother decorate the tiny evergreen tree.

"Don't forget to wrap up Babette's mouse," said Chatty, sadly. "Oh, Mother, are you *sure* Mr. Todd will come and see us before he goes, so I can give Babette her mouse and say good-bye to her?"

"I don't believe Mr. Todd would go away without saying good-bye," said her mother. "Now do close your eyes, dear, and try to go to sleep. Just think—when you wake up in the morning it will be Christmas!"

Usually Chatty woke up early in the morning, but the next day she slept soundly until quite late, and would have slept still longer if her mother had not awakened her.

"Chatty, Chatty! Wake up, darling! It's Christmas, Chatty, and here's a big surprise for you!"

Chatty sat up, rubbing her eyes, and looked over at the mantel where her stocking was dangling. Last night it had hung thin and limp, but now it was excitingly fat and lumpy. Above it on the mantel the tiny tree shone bravely with its electric lights and glittery ornaments. And on each

"Some darling kittens
at the A & P—
black, with white noses."

side of it were heaped packages wrapped in red tissue paper and tied with silver ribbon.

"Oh!" cried Chatty, and she hopped out of bed in her little flowered pyjamas and started across the room.

"No, darling—over here," said her mother. "*Here's* your surprise!"

"Merry Christmas, Chatty!" shouted Mr. Todd from the doorway. He was smiling broadly and he had a big square package in his hands, done up handsomely in tissue paper and red ribbon.

"Open it, Chatty, open it quickly, and let's see what's in it!" urged her mother as Mr. Todd placed the package carefully on the table. There was a scratching noise inside, and a muffled *mew!*

"Oh, Mr. Todd!" gulped Chatty as she tore off the ribbon and tissue paper with trembling hands. Off flew the lid before she could touch it, and out popped—*Babette.*

"She is yours to keep, this time, Chatty," beamed Mr. Todd, "I'm taking Cellophane with me, but Babette is too young to travel, so I want you to have her."

So after all it turned out to be the best Christmas Chatty had ever had. And besides Babette the presents she got were:

a doll and a book and a new dress from her mother
red mittens from her grandmother
a pink tea-set from her auntie
and a box of hankies with Minnie Mouses on them from her little cousins.

The next day Mr. Todd and Cellophane got on the train and went away.

But Babette stayed with Chatty and was her very own cat.